FINLEY FINDS A FRIEND

LAUREN WYCKOFF
ILLUSTRATED BY CHRISTOPHER ABLES

Archway Publishing books may be ordered through booksellers or by contacting:

Archway Publishing
1663 Liberty Drive
Bloomington, IN 47403
www.archwaypublishing.com
1 (888) 242-5904

ISBN: 978-1-4808-5670-7 (sc)
ISBN: 978-1-4808-5671-4 (hc)
ISBN: 978-1-4808-5669-1 (e)

Print information available on the last page.

Archway Publishing rev. date: 12/11/2017

ARCHWAY
PUBLISHING

Finley is a sweet and silly dog.

She loves to run and play.

Though she usually plays alone.

At night she sleeps in the forest
near her favorite park.

All alone.

She's scared of the dark at night.

She fears there are monsters in the shadows.

During the day Finley tries to play with
children and dogs at the park.

But people yell at Finley to stay
away because she is a pit bull.

They think she will be mean and
this makes Finley sad.

Sometimes she wishes she were a
different dog so people would like her.

One day, near dusk, a boy and his friends
are playing fetch in the park.

The boy throws the ball and it
rolls far into the forest.

He runs along on his own to find it.

The forest is dark and the boy gets lost.

Finley hears distant sobs and goes in search of whomever is crying.

Finley discovers the little boy
all alone, under a tree.

It's dark and Finley knows he must be
scared of the monsters, just like she is.

At first the boy thinks Finley is a
monster too. "Stay away!" he yells.

But Finley cautiously crawls to the
boy and gently licks his hand.

The boy sees she is a friendly dog.

Bravely they huddle in the dark together,
keeping an eye out for monsters.

Together, they are not scared.

Suddenly, a sound pierces the darkness.

At first, they think it is a monster
coming to gobble them up.

They hear the monster calling the boy's name.

"Tommy!"

A shadow moves toward them.

Finley squeaks out a sound to try
and scare away the monster.

Suddenly, the boy jumps up and runs towards the voice - leaves and twigs fly beneath his feet.

It's the boy's parents!

They found him!

Finley watches the little boy's
parents hug and kiss him.

She is glad the little boy isn't scared anymore.

She is also sad.

Finley's new friend is leaving her.

The family starts to walk away but the boy stops.

He looks at his parents, then back at Finley.

"What about my friend? We can't leave her alone in the dark forest," the boy says.

"Come home with us, girl," they say, smiling.

Finely can't believe it!

Finley found a home, with a family
who loves her just as she is.

CPSIA information can be obtained
at www.ICGtesting.com
Printed in the USA
BVHW05s2237090318
509997BV00020B/313/P